Pale

by

Chris Wooding

First American edition published in 2012 by Stoke Books,
an imprint of Barrington Stoke Ltd

18 Walker Street, Edinburgh, United Kingdom, EH3 7LP

www.stokebooks.com

Copyright © 2012 Chris Wooding

A catalog record for this book is available from
the US Library of Congress

Distributed in the United States and Canada by Lerner Publisher
Services, a division of Lerner Publishing Group, Inc.

241 First Avenue North, Minneapolis, MN 55401

www.lernerbooks.com

ISBN 978-1-78112-091-0

Printed in China

Contents

Chapter 1

A Lesson

We got the Pale on his way to school.

"Where do you think you're going?" asked Kyle. The way he said it, it wasn't a question. It was a threat.

The Pale kid looked around for help. There was nobody. We were on a wooded lane, hidden by trees on both sides. The lane was a short-cut between the school and the Graveyard. That was what they called the place where the Pales lived. The Graveyard. Most people thought they should stay there.

The Pale was a weedy little thing, about our age. He had that sick look that all the Pales did. His skin was so white, you could see blue veins underneath. His hair was white, too. And he had those strange eyes. His irises weren't blue or green or brown. They were white, too.

See why we call them Pales?

"Please," he moaned. "I don't want any trouble."

"What are you doing out of the Graveyard, Pale?" Kyle asked him. Kyle was a big kid. Much bigger than the Pale. Bigger than me, too.

The Pale started to back away. "I was going to school."

"Hear that, Jed?" Kyle asked me.

"Yeah," I said. "Wrong answer, Pale. School is for normal kids like us. It's not for Pales."

"But my dad says I have to go to school," the Pale said.

"Well *my* dad says you shouldn't," I replied. "He says it should be against the law. And he's a lawyer, so he should know."

Kyle grinned at me. Then in a flash, he went for the Pale kid and grabbed him by the arm. The kid did his best to get away, but Kyle was too strong. He pulled him over and pushed him down to the ground.

"This is what happens to Pales that stray out of the Graveyard," he said, and he started to punch the kid.

The Pale began to sob and beg. "Please! Don't!"

God. What a wimp. Pales make me sick.

So I started to punch and kick him too. He just lay there with his arms over his head. He didn't try to fight back. Just cried and squealed.

Pales. None of them have any guts.

"Hold him down, Jed," said Kyle. I grabbed the kid's arms and pinned him to the floor. His skin felt cold. His nose was running with snot and his eyes were tight shut. He was wailing really loud. I wanted to hit him just to shut him up.

Then I saw Kyle pick up a tree branch that had fallen on the path. It was heavy, like a club. He came back, and stood next to me. He was panting. There was a nasty look in his eye.

Kyle patted the club. "Let's teach him a *real* lesson."

"Hey!" I said, alarmed. "We just want to rough him up a bit. We don't want to kill him!"

"I'm going to make sure he never comes to school again," said Kyle. "Just hold him there for a minute." But there was something in his voice that scared me.

Kyle raised his club. He aimed for the Pale's head.

I couldn't believe he was really going to do it. He was joking, right? He just wanted to scare the Pale.

Didn't he?

Just at that second the Pale wriggled out of my grip, like a slimy little eel. Maybe I wasn't holding him tight enough. Or maybe I didn't want to hold him anymore. Not with Kyle about to smash his head in.

"Get him!" Kyle shouted, but the Pale was fast. He scampered away up the lane, faster than we could follow.

Kyle turned on me, furious. "You let him go!"

I dusted myself down. "He's learned his lesson," I said. "He won't be back."

Kyle snorted. "He'd better not be."

Kyle stalked off up the lane towards school. I followed after him. He wouldn't be mad at me for long. We were best friends, after all. It was just that he really, really hated Pales.

You couldn't blame him, though. Dead kids shouldn't be allowed to go to school.

Chapter 2
The Lazarus Serum

It all started when they invented the Lazarus Serum. A drug that can bring you back to life. But don't get your hopes up that you can use it to bring back your dead grandpa or anything. They have to give it to you right after you die. And it only works if you haven't been hurt too badly. If you've had your head chopped off, you're dead, and that's that.

There are some side effects. The drug turns your hair and skin white. It gives you those spooky eyes, too. No one's sure why. But at least it makes Pales easy to spot.

Once you've had the serum, your heart stops beating. You don't need to breathe anymore. You're dead. Only the serum lets you keep on going. Like a vampire or a zombie. And you stop getting older, too. Nobody's sure, but they say Pales can live forever.

Sounds pretty good, right?

Wrong.

The thing is, the drug only works on some people. You need to have the right blood type. Only one person in ten can come back as a Pale. The rest just have to die.

That makes a lot of people jealous. Why should Pales get a second chance when they don't?

The other thing is, it's selfish to live forever. I mean, there's not enough room on the planet for everyone as it is. There's not enough energy or food. So it's not fair to take more than your share. You die, time's up. That's how it should be.

Plus, there's a lot of religious people who don't like Pales. They think that God decides when you die, and so Pales are cheating. That gets them mad.

So it might sound like a good idea to come back as a Pale. But it's not. Because half the world hates you.

Chapter 3
The Missing Boy

It was lunch break on the day Kyle tried to kill the Pale. We always met up at the same spot in the yard at lunch. Me, Kyle, the twins and Sadie. Sadie was my girlfriend. Everyone knew she was the hottest girl in school. And she was with me.

I was first to arrive. There were some younger kids there, but I told them to get lost. Kyle turned up a minute later. He was in a good mood again. He'd forgotten all about what happened that morning.

But I remembered. He'd been about to bash in that Pale kid's head with a branch. I'd never seen him like that before.

"You were only messing around, right?" I asked him. "You weren't really going to kill him?"

"Nah," said Kyle. "I was just giving him a scare."

I wasn't sure if I believed him.

The twins turned up next. Nate and Ash. They were pushing each other and joking. I'd known the twins since I was five. We all used to hang out in elementary school. We'd been friends pretty much all our lives.

Sadie came last. My Sadie. She ran up, threw her arms around me, and gave me a kiss. Whenever we met, she always acted like she hadn't seen me for ages.

"Get a room, for God's sake," said one of the twins with a grin. I wasn't sure which one it was. I could never tell them apart.

Sadie stuck her tongue out at him. "Deal with it."

It felt really good to have Sadie in my arms. When I held her, I could forget all about the boring lessons I'd sat through. Math. God.

Me and Sadie had been together two years now. I hoped we'd be together forever. I would never admit it to my friends, but I really cared about her. And she cared about me. I could tell.

We were all messing around and talking when Mr. Grayson came over. He was a miserable old man. Every school has one teacher everyone hates. Mr. Grayson was ours.

"Alright, Mr. G?" said Kyle. He liked to be cocky.

Mr. Grayson didn't rise to it. He fixed us all with a cold glare. "Have any of you seen David Bloom at school today, by any chance?"

"Never heard of him," I said.

"Don't be stupid, Jed," said Mr. Grayson. "He's one of your classmates."

"Is he a Pale?" Kyle asked.

Mr. Grayson gave him a hard stare. "You know very well not to use that word, Kyle," he said. "If you mean 'is he one of the Returned?' then yes. He is."

You see, you weren't supposed to call Pales Pales. For some reason, people thought it was an insult. You were supposed to call them the Returned. Because they'd Returned from the dead – get it? But everyone called them Pales anyway.

"David Bloom didn't come to school today," Mr. Grayson went on. "His father doesn't know where he is. He's very worried." He looked at me and Kyle. "I don't suppose you two had anything to do with this, did you?"

Now I knew who Grayson was talking about. He meant the kid we'd beaten up on the way to school. I was in some classes with him, but I never knew his name. He was just a Pale.

"David Bloom," Kyle said. "Don't know him, Mr. Grayson. He sounds like a pansy to me."

Everyone cracked up at that. Except Mr. Grayson, of course. He snorted in disgust and walked away.

"I heard what happened to that kid," said Sadie, after Mr. Grayson was gone. "They were a rich family, once, with a huge house. But there was a gas leak in the kitchen. Everyone died from the fumes. They brought back David and his dad, but not his mom. She didn't have the right blood type."

"He's rich? No kidding?" Kyle asked. I could tell he was thinking of stealing the Pale kid's lunch money.

"Not anymore," said Sadie. "The lawyers took everything. In the end they had to go and live in the Graveyard with the rest of the Pales."

"Bet it was your dad that took the money!" one of the twins said to me.

"Bet it was," I said. I was so proud.

There were a lot of lawyers like my dad. Afterlife lawyers, they were called. Their job was to take everything they could from the Pales. You see, the law said a Pale was dead even though they were still walking around. They didn't have any rights. That meant their relatives could take all their stuff. A good lawyer could take everything a Pale owned from them. And my dad was a *great* lawyer.

Even if a Pale managed to keep hold of their stuff, they soon ended up poor. Not many people wanted to give a Pale a job. No one wanted to do business with them. Sooner or later, they all went to the Graveyard, where they belonged.

I lifted my head and saw a group of Pales on the other side of the schoolyard. They stood in a cluster, keeping their heads down. The Pales at school all hung out together. It was creepy.

"Don't they make your skin crawl?" asked Sadie. She shivered and pressed herself up close to me. "The way they sneak around in gangs like that?"

One of the twins gave her a nudge. "That might be you, one day," he said with an evil grin. "After all, you've got the right blood type, haven't you? So has Jed. You've been tested like all of us."

He was right. Everyone got tested to see if the Lazarus Serum would work on them. Me and Sadie had the right blood type. The other three didn't. I wondered if that was the reason Kyle hated Pales so much.

Sadie made a face. "Eww! No! I would never want to come back as one of them."

"What about you?" Kyle asked me. "What if you had to make a choice?" He was staring at me hard.

"Me? A Pale?" I said. "I'd rather die."

Chapter 4
Falling, Like in a Dream

I was walking with Sadie after school when my dad pulled up in his car. It was a shiny new BMW.

"Need a lift?" he asked.

"No, thanks," I said. "We're going to see a movie. I'll be back home later."

"Sounds good," he said with a smile. "Hi, Sadie. How's everything?"

"Everything's great," she said. She held my hand and looked at me.

"Oh, Jed, I forgot," said my dad. "I got us those tickets for the game on Saturday. Box seats, of course. Best in the stadium."

"Nice one, Dad," I said. "You're the best!"

My dad winked. "You just have to know the right people," he said. "See you later." And he drove off.

"You're so lucky to have a dad like that," Sadie told me. "My dad's just embarrassing. I wouldn't be seen dead with him."

"Yeah," I said. My dad was pretty cool. We did a lot of stuff together. All the other dads I knew were like Sadie's – boring and old. But I thought the world of mine. He was more like a friend than a dad.

As we walked on down the road to the movies, Sadie chatted about school and stuff. She was always so happy when she was with me.

I was thinking about how good she made me feel too as we stepped out into the road. I wasn't paying attention to anything else. Maybe that was why I didn't see the car until it was too late.

It was coming way too fast. Heading straight for Sadie. I heard the screech of brakes.

Then I moved. I dived forward and shoved her, hard. I pushed her out of the way of the car.

It hit me instead.

It was like I was a fly getting swatted by a giant metal hand. The blow stunned me. White light exploded behind my eyes. I went flying through the air. Then I was falling, like in a dream.

I hit the tarmac, and everything went black.

Chapter 5
What the Accident Did

I opened my eyes. Things were fuzzy at first. I blinked. Every part of my body hurt.

"Look," said my mom's voice. "He's awake."

Mom was just a blurred figure next to me. I was in a bed. Crisp sheets. The room smelled cool and clean.

It took a minute to realize where I was. I was in hospital.

Dad was standing over on the other side of the room, by the door. At least, I thought it was Dad. He was too far away to see very well.

"Dad?" I croaked. My throat was so dry.

Mom took my hand. "Sssh," she said. "Don't tire yourself."

I remembered being hit by the car. "Is ... is Sadie OK?"

"Huh!" said my dad from the other side of the room. "She's just fine." He said it like he was angry about it.

I didn't understand. Dad had always been fond of Sadie. But at least she was OK.

My eyes had adjusted to the light now, so I could see a little better. I could see Mom's face. She looked so worried. That made *me* worried. How badly had I been hurt?

I wiggled my toes under the covers. I bent my legs. I shifted about a bit.

It hurt, but not too much. No bones broken.

So why was Mom looking so worried?

"Dad?" I said again. "Am I OK?"

He snorted, as if that was a stupid question. I didn't get it. Dad was always so nice to me. Why was he being so mean?

"You had an accident," said Mom, patting my hand.

"I know, Mom. Am I OK, though?"

"It was a very *bad* accident," she said, and she started to cry.

Now I was really scared. I thought they'd be happy that I hadn't been killed. But they didn't seem happy at all. Something was very wrong.

"Dad?" I asked. "Why are you standing all the way over there?"

"I just ..." he began. But then he didn't seem to know what to say. "Forget it," he said. Then he pulled open the door and walked out of the room.

I was shocked. Why was he treating me this way?

"He'll come around," said Mom. "It's hard for him. With his job, you know. People are going to talk."

"Talk about what?"

She closed her eyes. "The accident ... Jed, it was really bad ..." She opened her bag, took out a mirror and gave it to me.

My eyes had cleared now. Enough so I could see the face in the mirror, looking back at me.

It was my face, but different, ugly. My hair had gone white. My cheeks had no color, and you could see small blue veins underneath. My eyes were spooky. It was like seeing the ghost of myself.

But I wasn't a ghost. I was something worse.

I was a Pale.

Chapter 6
Five Big Letters

Sadie did it. She made me a Pale.

When the ambulance came, I was already dead. They didn't have much time. So they asked Sadie what I would have wanted. And Sadie told them to bring me back.

What I didn't understand was why. Why did she do it? She knew I didn't want to be a Pale, and she got them to bring me back anyway. That question tore me up. Why didn't she just let me die?

It would have been better than living as a Pale.

After I got out of the hospital, I stayed off school for a few days. But things at home were hard. Dad didn't even look at me. Mom tried to be nice, but I could tell she was sad. I heard her crying when she thought I wasn't around.

I didn't feel any different to the way I was before. I still felt like the same old Jed inside. But Mom and Dad didn't think I was the same. When they looked at me they saw a Pale. A Pale that looked like their dead son.

I couldn't stand being at home. It was making me too sad. So I went back to school.

Dad used to drop me off in his car in the mornings. But he didn't want to do it anymore. It would look bad. He was an Afterlife lawyer, after all. His job was to take stuff from Pales. What would people say if they knew his own son was a Pale?

So I walked instead.

It wasn't easy, going to my first class. Everyone stared at me. They'd all heard what had happened. I tried to stare back at them, to defy them. I was still the same Jed they'd known a few days ago! But I couldn't help looking down at my feet. I felt so small. I knew what they thought of me.

Our first class of the day was with Mr. Grayson. He just looked at me as I sat down. He didn't say anything, but there was a little smirk on his face. Then he wrote on the board. Five big letters.

"'KARMA,'" he said. "Today, class, we're going to learn the meaning of the word 'KARMA.'"

Nobody spoke to me all morning. It was like they didn't know what to do with me. The second class was worse than the first. I felt like I didn't belong in my seat. I wanted to go home, but home was just as bad.

At lunch break, I went to the spot where we always met. They were all there. Kyle, Sadie and the twins. They were laughing and joking. I walked over to them.

One of the twins saw me coming. He nudged the others, and they stopped laughing. Kyle's face went hard.

"What do you think you're doing?" he said, as I joined them.

"What do you mean?" I asked.

He pointed to the group of Pales on the other side of the schoolyard. They were muttering to each other and looking at me. "That's where you belong now," Kyle said.

I couldn't believe it. "Kyle!" I said. "It's me – Jed! Remember? Your best friend!"

Kyle shook his head. He looked really angry. "Jed died. He was hit by a car. You ... you're just a Pale."

"I didn't want to be a Pale!" I shouted. I pointed at Sadie. "She brought me back!"

Sadie began to cry.

"Look what you've done!" Kyle said. "Get out of here!"

I ignored him. "Sadie!" I said. "Look at me! Why did you do it?"

"Leave her alone!" one of the twins shouted. He grabbed my arm, but I shook him off.

"Stay out of this!" I said, "She's my girlfriend!" I stared at Sadie. "Why did you do it?"

"Because I loved you!" she said. There were tears running down her face. "Because I couldn't stand to lose you!"

I couldn't speak for a minute. She loved me? It was the first time she'd ever said it. It was the first time any girl had said it to me.

Sadie turned away. "Anyway, it doesn't matter now," she said.

"It doesn't matter?" I shouted. "How can you say it doesn't matter?"

Sadie wiped her eyes. "It doesn't matter, because you're a Pale. We can't ever be together now. It just wouldn't work."

"You're breaking up with me?" I said. "You brought me back to life, you made me a Pale, and now you're breaking up with me?"

Kyle stepped between us. "You heard her," he said. "It's over."

"Get out of my way!" I said. I tried to get past him, but he shoved me away. Hard. I tripped and fell to the ground.

"Jed is dead," Kyle said. "Go hang out with your Pale friends."

I lay there, stunned. My friends were looking at me like I was an enemy. My girlfriend had turned her back on me. Some kids nearby were laughing at me, there on the ground. They would never have dared to laugh at me before. The Pale kids watched me from the other side of the schoolyard. They could sense they were about to get a new member for their creepy little gang.

"I'm not like those guys!" I shouted at Kyle. "I'm different!"

"Are you?" he asked. "Funny. You all look the same to me."

I couldn't take it anymore. I got to my feet and ran. Out of the schoolyard and out of the school. I didn't know where I was going. I just wanted to run. I kept running till I couldn't run any longer.

When I stopped, I found myself on a wooded lane. I knew it at once. It was the same place we'd beaten up David Bloom a few days ago. The shortcut between the school and the Graveyard.

Why had I come here, I wondered?

And then it hit me. I had nowhere else to go. I wasn't wanted at home. I wasn't wanted at school. There was only one place where people like me belonged.

I hung my head and started walking down the lane.

Towards the Graveyard.

Chapter 7
The Graveyard

It was the middle of the afternoon when I reached the Graveyard. It was a dirty, run-down part of the city. A slum where nobody ever went. Nobody except Pales, anyway.

I walked with hunched shoulders and kept my head down. It was scary to be surrounded by so many Pales. I felt like they knew I wasn't really one of them. Like they would see me and know I shouldn't be there.

Everything was shabby. The windows had a layer of grime on them. Litter blew down the street. Pales wandered here and there, wearing cheap gear. Stuff from outlet places and Good Will. Some of them looked like bums.

It wasn't like home. Mom and Dad lived in a nice street, lined with trees. We had a big house. The garbage truck came on time. You never saw a bum there, Pale or not.

I wanted to go back there so badly. But I couldn't. I couldn't face Dad. And I didn't want to make Mom cry.

But now I was here, I had no idea what to do. I just walked around. I looked in the windows of empty shops. I kicked stones that had fallen off ruined buildings. I tried not to look anyone in the eye.

In the end I sat down in a shop doorway. The shop was closed, like all the shops here. No one had any money.

It was getting cold and dark. I was only wearing my school clothes. I began to shiver. I was hungry, too.

Until that moment, I didn't think Pales felt hunger or cold. I just thought they were like zombies. The undead. But now I knew.

Nothing was different after you died. Nothing except the way people treated you.

The whole thing made me angry. How could Sadie do this to me? She would have been dead if I hadn't saved her. Instead it was me who died. It wasn't fair!

I was the same Jed she loved before I was hit by that car. It was only the outside that had changed. But she couldn't see that. She only saw a Pale.

Why didn't she just leave me dead? It would have been better than this!

In a while night fell. I was getting really cold. I needed to move, to keep warm. I could smell food cooking somewhere, so I went to find it.

The Graveyard was all yellow light and black shadows under the street-lamps. In the middle of one road, I found a soup kitchen. Pales were lining up with bowls. Three women were giving them broth and dumplings. Normal women, not Pales. What were they doing in the Graveyard?

I got in line. I was too hungry to be afraid now. It freaked me out to have Pales standing so close to me. But I wanted that food.

I didn't speak to anyone until I got to the front. One of the women looked down at me. "Where's your bowl?" she asked.

"I don't have one," I said.

She gave me a kind smile. "You're new, eh?" Then she found me a bowl, and filled it up. She put in an extra dumpling.

"That'll keep you going," she said, winking.

I mumbled a thank you and shuffled off. It was strange to see normal people being nice to Pales. I was used to people picking on them, the way I did.

I took my bowl and headed towards some tables by the side of the road. I planned to find a place to sit on my own. But then a group of Pales walked up to me. Three older boys, and one kid my age. A kid I knew.

"Remember me?" he said.

I did. It was David Bloom. The kid that me and Kyle beat up. I looked at his friends.

All of them were bigger than me.

The tables had turned now. I was on his turf. This wasn't going to go well.

"Listen, about what happened before," I said. "I'm ... sorry."

"Now you are," said David.

I knew what he meant. I wouldn't have been sorry if I hadn't died. I would have kept on beating up Pales.

I hung my head. "Well," I said. "Let's get this over with."

"Get what over with?" David asked.

"You've come for payback, right?" I asked.

David shook his head. "No," he said. "You're one of us now. We need to look out for each other. No one else is going to."

"I'm not one of you," I said. I still couldn't think of myself as a Pale.

"Everyone says that at first," David told me. He put his hand on my arm. "Come on – sit down. Eat with us. I don't know about you, but I'm hungry."

Chapter 8
Back to School

I stayed with David after that. He told his dad I was a friend from school. He never said anything about how I used to beat him up. His dad said I could stay for a while, if I wanted. I had to sleep on the floor, but it was better than nothing.

David looked after me for a whole week. He told me who people were. He showed me where to get warm clothes and meals for free. He let me hang out with him and his friends.

At first it was strange. I didn't feel like I was one of them. But they didn't mind me

being there. At first I hardly said anything.
After a while, I started joining in. Soon, it
didn't feel strange anymore.

All the time, I was thinking about Sadie.
Sadie, Sadie, Sadie. I think I must have been in
love with her all the time, like she said she was
in love with me. Even though I didn't know it.
Otherwise it wouldn't have hurt so much, what
she did.

After that first week at David's, his dad
told me I'd better go back to school.

"Being a Pale doesn't mean you have to give
up, Jed," he said. "You need to get an
education. You might be around for a long
time. In fact, you might be around forever.
But one day, there'll be more of us than them.
Then they won't be able to keep us in the
slums. So you'd better get ready for that day,
yeah? You'd better get smart."

I didn't want to, but I did what he said.

It was easier this time. I sat with the rest
of the Pales at the back of the class. I kept
quiet and stayed out of everyone's way.

Nobody took any notice of me. That was how I wanted it.

At lunch break, I hung out with the Pales.

The schoolyard felt dangerous. I knew there were kids who would beat me up, just for being a Pale. I used to be one of them. But when I was with David and his friends, I felt safe. I knew they wouldn't let anything happen to me. No wonder Pales hung out in gangs all the time. Everyone was out to get them.

On the other side of the schoolyard I could see Sadie and Kyle and the twins. They were hanging out in the usual spot. Kyle had his arm round Sadie. The sight made me burn up. It hadn't taken her long to get over me!

David saw where I was looking. "Forget her," he said. "You can't be her boyfriend now. Not unless she gets hit by a car, too."

And then I had an idea. An evil, genius idea.

"Hey," I said. "Don't they keep some Lazarus Serum at school? In the medical room?"

"Yeah," said David. "In case some kid at school dies. In case the ambulance can't get here in time."

"I know a way that me and Sadie can be together," I said. "But I'll need your help."

"Does it mean that much to you?" David asked.

"Yes!" I said.

"Alright," he said. "I'll help you." He looked at me. "What do you want me to do?"

"I need you to help me steal that serum."

Chapter 9

Two Thieves

It got dark early at this time of year. We waited till the last bell, then we sneaked into a classroom and hid. We listened as everyone else left the school. Voices shouted down the hallways. Footsteps passed by. All the lights in the classrooms were turned out.

Then there was no sound at all. Only our breathing. The silence was a bit creepy.

"I don't like this," said David. "We could get into a lot of trouble."

"You're dead," I reminded him. "What's the worst that could happen?"

We crept out of the classroom. The lights in the hallways were still on. I wondered if they left them on all night.

"This way," I said.

The medical room was where you went if you needed to see the school nurse. I'd been there a couple of times before. Once I got sick from the burgers in the cafeteria. That was when I'd asked the nurse what was in the medicine cabinet. "Lazarus Serum," she said. Just in case.

I could tell David was scared. So was I, but I didn't show it. I wasn't worried about getting expelled but I was worried about getting arrested. I'd be sent to a juvenile detention for sure. There was no such thing as a fair trial for a Pale. My dad told me that.

We reached the door. "Keep a lookout," I told David. "There might still be someone around."

David nodded, his face scared. I started to feel bad about asking him to come along. He was taking a big risk.

I wondered why he'd agreed. Maybe because it was the kind of thing a friend would do.

That stopped me in my tracks. I'd never really thought of him as a friend before.

"Hey," I said to him. "Thanks."

He looked surprised. "For what?"

I waved my hand around. "You know. Everything."

David shrugged, but I could tell he was kind of pleased. "You're welcome."

Then I opened the door to the medical room and went in.

It was dark in there, but there was light from the hallway outside. The medicine cabinet was on the far wall. I sneaked over to it and pulled the handle. It was locked. But I had come prepared. I pulled a long screwdriver out of my pocket. I'd stolen it from the design lab.

I stuck the screwdriver in between the cabinet doors. The lock wasn't too strong. I could force it off. I leaned on the screwdriver and the metal doors of the cabinet began to bend.

Then I heard something. Faint footsteps, coming up the hall.

Someone was in the school. Someone was coming.

"It's the janitor!" David whispered from the doorway. He looked scared.

I swore under my breath. Better make myself scarce until the janitor was gone.

But when I tried to pull the screwdriver out, it wouldn't come. It was stuck.

"Jed!" David said. "We have to go!"

"I can't leave the screwdriver here!" I hissed. "The janitor will see it!" I pulled at it again.

"Come on!" said David. He was frantic now.

I looked over my shoulder. "Shut the door," I said. "I'll meet you outside."

There was no time for him to argue. The footsteps were getting closer. The janitor was going to appear any minute. So David pulled the door to the medical room shut and ran away. I felt better once I knew he'd gone. I didn't want to get him into trouble. This whole thing was my idea, after all.

But there was still the problem of the screwdriver. If the janitor looked into the room, he'd see it sticking out of the cabinet. I couldn't pull it out. So there was only one thing to do. I put all my weight on it.

The lock broke with a loud crack, and the doors banged open.

The footsteps stopped. I held my breath.

"Is somebody there?" came a voice from the hallway.

Uh-oh.

The janitor had heard me. I looked around in a panic for somewhere to hide. There was nothing in the room but the cabinet, a little desk for the nurse, and a bed for sick kids. Could I hide under it? No. He'd see me from the door.

The footsteps started again. They were slow now. The janitor knew something was up. I could hear him open doors as he went.

"Hello?" he said. "Who is it? I know you're there."

I put the screwdriver in my pocket and opened the cabinet. There it was. The kind of needle they give you shots with. It was inside a plastic bag, which was marked "Lazarus Serum". I grabbed it and closed the cabinet. Unless you looked carefully, you couldn't see the broken lock. I just had to hope the janitor wouldn't look carefully.

He was almost outside now. I needed a place to hide. There wasn't one. So I did the best I could. I hid behind the door.

The janitor pushed the door open a second later. He peered into the dark room. I held my breath. The door was between me and him.

Light fell from the hallway onto the medicine cabinet. The cabinet door was slightly open. If he saw that, the game was up.

It seemed like ages that he stood there. He knew something was wrong. He'd heard something, but he didn't know what. Any moment I expected him to notice the broken cabinet.

But he didn't. He left the room and shut the door.

I breathed out in relief. I listened to his footsteps as they went away down the hallway. Then I took the needle of serum out of my pocket and looked at it. A smile spread across my face.

"This one's for you, Sadie," I said.

Chapter 10
Arrangements

I found David outside the school gate. We walked back to the Graveyard together, taking the back streets. Walking in the dark was risky for Pales. You always had to keep an eye out for normal kids. If they caught you, they'd beat you up. Just like I used to do.

David was really quiet.

"What's up?" I asked.

He shrugged.

"You don't have to feel bad for running off," I said. "I told you to, remember?"

"It's not that," he said. He kicked the ground with his toe. "What do you want the Lazarus Serum for?" he asked.

"I can't tell you," I said. "You'll just have to trust me."

"I'm not stupid," he said. "You want it for Sadie, don't you? You're going to turn her into a Pale."

I didn't answer.

"It's not right," he said.

"I'll tell you what's not right!" I snapped at him. "She brought me back to life and then she dumped me! She left me like this! A Pale!"

"Being a Pale isn't so bad," said David. "Sure, it can be hard. But would you rather be dead?"

A week ago I would have said yes. Now I wasn't so sure. I'd grown to like David and his friends. They were just like other kids. Except they were dead.

"Listen," I said. "That girl loved me. And ..." I swallowed. It wasn't easy to admit. "I think I might have loved her, too. So we're

47

going to be together." I held up the needle of serum. "I'm going to make her like us."

David just looked sad.

"I won't ask you to help anymore," I said. "Just don't try and stop me."

David didn't speak the rest of the way back. We parted at the border of the Graveyard. He went home. I wondered if he'd say anything to his dad about what I planned. But I didn't think he would. He wasn't the sort to tell on a friend.

In my pocket I found some coins I'd found by the side of the road. Then I went to find a telephone booth. I knew Sadie's phone number by heart.

"Hello?" she said, as she picked up the phone. The sound of her voice almost made me cry.

"Hi, Sadie," I said. "It's me."

I heard her give a little gasp. "Jed?" she asked.

"Right," I said.

It was like she didn't know what to say after that. "How are you?" she asked, in the end.

"Not so great, actually," I told her. "I ran away from home. I'm staying in the Graveyard now. Sleeping on someone's floor. What about you?"

She started to sob. I hated to hear her cry. "I'm sorry, Jed," she said. "It's just that ... Well, when I saw you at school ... With all those people around ... You understand, right?"

"Yeah," I said. "I understand."

"When I hear your voice on the phone, I can almost imagine you're alive again. The old Jed. Not a Pale."

"I *am* the old Jed," I said. "And I'm also a Pale."

There was silence from her end of the phone. We both knew what she couldn't say. Pales and normal kids couldn't be together.

"We need to talk," I said.

She sniffed. "OK."

"I want to see you," I said. "Face to face. You owe me that much."

"Alright," she said.

"There's this deserted old apartment building I know," I told her. "Nobody goes there. Nobody will see us together."

"Tonight?" she asked.

"Tonight," I said.

I told her how to get there and we agreed on a time. Then I put the phone down. I patted the needle of serum in my pocket.

"Tonight," I said again.

Chapter 11
A Secret Meeting

The apartments stood on the edge of some waste ground. They were all boarded up and abandoned. It looked like no one had lived in them for years.

I crept towards them across the waste ground. Away from the street-lamps, it was very dark. I was nervous. If my heart could beat, it would have been hammering. I kept on thinking I could hear footsteps following me. But whenever I looked back, I didn't see anything.

I was scared of seeing Sadie again. I was scared I wouldn't be able to do what I had to.

It wasn't murder. That's what I told myself. If I gave her the serum, she'd die. That was true. But she wouldn't be dead dead. She'd be like me. And I was alive. My heart didn't beat, and I didn't need to breathe, but I was alive.

So it couldn't be murder.

But then I started to wonder. What was I really doing this for? Was it truly because I loved her? Or was it all to get her back for what she did? Because she had turned me into a Pale and then dumped me?

I wasn't sure. I didn't know if I could go through with it. I just wanted to talk to her again, face to face. Without Kyle or anyone else around.

The thought of Kyle made me angry. I remembered him with his arm round Sadie. That wasn't what best friends were meant to do. I'd only been gone a few days and they were already together.

Maybe, if I talked to her, she'd see past the white skin and the strange eyes. Maybe she'd see that I was just me. Maybe she'd be my girlfriend again.

Fat chance.

I reached the building. The door had been boarded up, but the boards had been broken. It was me and Kyle who did that, back when we were friends. We'd gone out to explore together. It all seemed a long time ago now.

I went inside.

It was cold. Thick shadows gathered in the hallways. Water dripped from somewhere above me. There was crap lying all around.

I climbed the stairs and went into the apartment at the top. I knew I'd be able to get inside. Me and Kyle had broken the door down last time we were here.

I was right. The door was half off its hinges. I went in.

The apartment was probably shabby even before it was abandoned. Now it was foul. The carpet was mouldy. The wallpaper was peeling. Everything stank of rot.

Not the best place to meet a girl. But at least there'd be nobody around. No one to see what I was going to do.

I took the Lazarus needle out of my pocket. Faint light from outside shone on the serum. Could I really do it to her? Could I make her a Pale like me?

If I did, then she would have to be mine and not Kyle's.

If I didn't, then I had to give her up forever.

I heard a voice. "Jed? Are you here?" It was her. She was downstairs. I put the needle back in my pocket as fast as I could.

"I'm up here," I called.

"Where?" she asked. I could hear she was coming up the stairs.

"The apartment at the top."

I could hear movement down below. I stood there and waited. After a short while, she appeared in the door of the apartment.

She looked amazing. Even though she was all bundled up in a coat. We stared at each other. Her eyes were so sad.

I knew, right at that moment, that I could never hurt her. I couldn't turn her into a Pale. She'd saved me, after all. I would have died if it wasn't for her. It hurt that she'd turned her back on me, but I understood. She just couldn't face being with a Pale.

Maybe I would have done the same, if it had been her that died.

"Sadie," I said. "It's good to see you again."

But she didn't seem happy to see me. Tears were running down her face.

"What's wrong?" I asked.

"I'm sorry," she whispered.

And then she stepped aside to let Kyle step through the doorway. Kyle and the twins.

They were carrying baseball bats. And they were staring right at me.

Chapter 12
Ambush

"What's this?" said Kyle. "Seems we've got a Pale here. Should have stayed in the Graveyard, Pale."

I backed away from them. Kyle stepped into the apartment. The twins were behind him. Sadie was trying to see past them, scared.

"Sadie!" I called to her. "Why?"

"I don't know," she said. "I just told him. I couldn't help it. I didn't know he'd get so mad. I didn't want anyone to get hurt!"

"Shut your mouth!" Kyle snapped at her. "It's a bit late for that. You've done your bit. If you don't want to stick around, get lost."

Sadie backed away at the tone of his voice. She gave me one last look, and turned and ran down the stairs.

I should have known she'd tell Kyle I called. She never could keep a secret.

Kyle was carrying a big plastic bottle in one hand. He put it down by the door. I heard it slosh with liquid. But I didn't have time to wonder what was inside. Kyle and the twins were coming towards me.

"We're not too fond of Pales trying to steal our girls," said Kyle.

His face was twisted in hate. I'd never had anyone look at me like that before. He looked like he wanted to kill me.

"I just wanted to talk to her," I said. "She was my girlfriend for years. I just wanted to – "

Kyle swung his bat and smashed a rotten chair to pieces. The noise made me jump.

"Stop talking," he said. His voice was low and quiet. "Every word you say makes it worse. That's Jed's voice you're using. That's Jed's body you're wearing. He was my friend. But you! You're a Pale. A goddamned back-from-the-dead Pale. A walking corpse!"

Kyle shook his head. "You should have stayed dead," he said. "I'm gonna make you wish you had."

Then he ran at me and swung his bat.

"Kyle! Don't!" I shouted. I put my arm up to defend myself. The bat hit me on the hand with a horrible crack. Pain exploded through me like white fire. I tripped on the ragged carpet and fell backwards. I had barely hit the floor before Kyle kicked me in the ribs.

Then the twins joined in. I tried to cover my head, but the blows came from everywhere. Someone's boot caught me on the cheek. Stars of pain burst in my head. I couldn't move. Couldn't escape. Couldn't do anything but lie curled in a ball.

They kept on pounding me with bats and boots. In the end I lost track of time. One second seemed like forever. The pain kept coming. They hit me again and again. When were they going to stop? *Were* they going to stop?

Then they did stop. And that was worse. While they had been hitting me, the pain had been bad. But now they had stopped, I started to feel it ten times more. There were bruises all over my body. It felt like I'd broken some ribs, but it hurt too much to tell for sure. I coughed, and tasted blood on my swollen lips. One of my eyes was starting to swell, so the eyelid was half shut.

Kyle stood over me, panting. His teeth were gritted and he had an ugly expression on his face. He looked down at me. We'd been friends all our lives, but now he didn't know me at all.

"I'll show you what we do to Pales around here," he said.

He put a cigarette in his mouth and lit it. Kyle didn't even smoke, normally. Then he went and picked up the plastic bottle full of liquid. He pulled off the cap, and the apartment filled with the smell of it.

It was gasoline.

Horror clutched at my stomach.

He was going to set fire to me.

I started to struggle, trying to get away.
But the twins held me down. Kyle came closer.
The tip of the cigarette glowed.

"You're gonna burn, Pale," he said.

"No!" I screamed. But I couldn't stop him.
The twins had my arms and legs pinned down.

"You sure about this?" one of them asked
Kyle. "I think he's learned his lesson."

"We keep beating them up, and they keep
coming back!" Kyle snarled. "Someone needs to
do something. Now hold him still!"

The twins didn't like it, but they did what
he said. Everyone always did what Kyle said.
Even me, before I died.

He stood over me. He tipped up the bottle
to pour the gasoline on me.

Then there was a shout, and the sound of
running footsteps. Five kids came rushing into

the room. Pale kids. And leading them was David.

David threw himself at Kyle, even though Kyle was much bigger than him. Kyle was taken by surprise. He tripped against me and fell over. The bottle flew out of his hand. Oil glugged out of it and spread across the carpet.

The twins tried to defend themselves, but the Pales were all over them, kicking and punching. I felt David's hands on me, pulling me to my feet. Kids were fighting all around me.

I saw Kyle's cigarette, where it had fallen from his mouth. I saw the gasoline spread towards it.

"Watch it!" I cried, but too late. The gasoline reached the lit cigarette. And the bottle exploded.

I was thrown back to the ground. When I got up, there was fire everywhere. Kyle was screaming and beating at himself. The arm of his coat was on fire. Everyone was in a panic. They'd forgotten about fighting each other. Half the room had gone up in flames!

Kyle ran screaming out of the apartment. He was still trying to put out the fire on his arm. The twins looked at one another and then ran after him.

I could feel the terrible heat from the flames. I wondered what it would have felt like, if it had been me that was on fire.

"Come on!" said David. "Don't just stand there staring!"

"You followed me," I said. "You all followed me here."

"Well," David grinned. "We had to make sure you were OK, didn't we?"

I suddenly wanted to throw my arms around him. So I did.

"Hey! Easy now!" he said.

But I couldn't help it. Because I knew now that he was my friend. And so were all the others, the Pales who'd risked their lives to help me. They weren't like Kyle and the twins, or even Sadie. They were the real thing. The kind who'd stick with you, no matter what.

"Let's get out of here," I said. "We're done."

Chapter 13
The Last Goodbye

But I wasn't done. Not yet.

We ran outside and got far enough away to be safe from the fire. Then we hid in the waste ground and watched that place burn. My whole body hurt, but I still felt good. It could have been much, much worse. If it wasn't for my friends.

The flames had spread so fast. Already the roof of the building was on fire, and I could see smoke coming from the top floor windows. There was no sign of Kyle or the twins.

"So I suppose Sadie never showed up?" David asked.

"She showed up," I said. "She was the one who led them here."

David frowned. "Where did she go, then?"

"She ran off," I said.

"Are you sure?" he asked. "Because we were right behind you. And we didn't see anyone come out."

I stared at the burning building. Fear nearly made my heart stop. "You think she's still in there?" I asked.

David shrugged. "Maybe."

Suddenly I found I was running. Back towards the building.

"Stop!" David shouted after me. "It's too dangerous!"

But it didn't matter. Whatever Sadie had done to me, I couldn't leave her in there.

I pushed my way into the burning building. I was holding my side with one hand to keep my cracked ribs from stopping me. My whole body was a mass of pain. I could only see out of one eye. Smoke and poisonous fumes filled the hallways.

I should have started coughing. I should have got dizzy from the fumes. But I was a Pale. I didn't need to breathe.

I went up the stairs. The apartment where the fire had started was at the top. I knew Sadie wasn't there. So I checked the apartment on the floor below. The door was closed, but not locked. I tried to open it. It was jammed.

I kicked it in.

Sadie was in there. It was hard to see her with all the smoke. She was lying on the floor, face down.

In an instant, I knew what had happened. She hadn't wanted to see me get beaten up, so she had hid in here and pulled the door shut. But it was an old door, and it had got jammed. The smoke from the fire had made her pass out.

I picked her up and carried her down the stairs and outside. David and the others had just got to the building. They helped me take her down the road, away from the building. We laid her down on the sidewalk.

Her eyes were shut. She'd breathed in too much smoke. I looked at her as she lay there. It was weird, but I didn't feel anything. Not love, not hate. Nothing.

The road was deserted, but we could hear sirens in the distance.

"Well?" said David. "If you want to go through with your plan, now's your chance."

I took the Lazarus needle out of my pocket. He was right. I could turn Sadie into a Pale right here and now. Nobody would know that she hadn't really died. Even she wouldn't know. She'd wake up as a Pale, and I'd have saved her. Then she'd have to be my girlfriend again.

Except that I didn't want to do that. I didn't want her. I didn't want anything to do with my old life anymore.

"She doesn't deserve to be one of us," I said. And I put the needle down next to her on the ground. The paramedics could use it on someone who needed it.

David smiled and slapped me on the arm. The other Pales grinned and patted me on the back.

"Let's get going before the police and ambulance get here," David said. "She'll be OK. But if they see a bunch of Pales near a burning building …"

I got to my feet and gave Sadie one last look.

"See you sometime," I said to her. "Or maybe not."

And with that, we ran. Across the waste ground, back to the Graveyard. Behind us, the sirens got louder and louder and louder.